CW01667922

From Out of the Wind

From Out of the Wind

Marc C. Lee

Pad 39 Press
Los Angeles, California

All illustrations by the author
Front cover image and inside photos by the author
Editing by Jenny DePierre

First paperback edition, September 2022

ISBN: 979-8-218-03629-4 (softcover)
Library of Congress Control Number: 2022912724

Printed in the United States of America

Published by Pad 39 Press
Los Angeles, California
Visit www.pad39press.com or contact agent@pad39press.com

Dedication

To my flight students, for sharing the beauty and mystery of flight with me, and for letting me learn from each of you.

Because I Fly

By Grover C. Norwood

Because I fly

I laugh more than other men

I look up an see more than they,

I know how the clouds feel,

What it's like to have the blue in my lap,

to look down on birds,

to feel freedom in a thing called the stick...

who but I can slice between God's billowed legs,

and feel then laugh and crash with His step

Who else has seen the unclimbed peaks?

The rainbow's secret?

The real reason birds sing?

Because I Fly,

I envy no man on earth.

Preface

The story you are about to read is based on my experiences ferrying a Grumman AA-1 aircraft from Texas to California with its owner in late November 2021. I have fictionalized certain elements to protect the privacy of individuals, and I have included vignettes that were told to me by other pilots who, after hearing my story, shared their own experiences. It is therefore presented as a work of fiction. Even so, the next time you look up and trace some winged machine across the sky, know that unexplained mysteries still exist in its farthest corners.

- Marc C. Lee

Rancho Santa Margarita, California
August 2022

CHAPTER 1

1,029.

By itself it was just a number, without meaning or relevance. If it had been miles, the number could mean no distance at all, or an odyssey. To a sailboat captain, it would represent weeks of navigation and provisions and weather. To a satellite tracker, it would translate to 3.6 minutes of orbital travel. And to the pilot of a light airplane suspended a mile above an infinite expanse of desert, it would come to mean something more. That discovery still lay ahead of me at this hour.

The 1970's Panasonic clock-radio jarred me from an awful sleep and doubled my heart rate in an instant with its mechanical alarm. It woke me with the subtlety of a cattle prod into a black void that was unnerving. Early mornings have always been my enemy, and a glance at the luminous dials on my watch confirmed my disorientation: It was 5:30 am.

I had spent an uneasy, fitful night in a windowless airplane hangar somewhere in East Texas on a collection of springs and sags and torture devices somebody had deemed a "mattress." I was in a dry-walled cube known as *Pilot's Sleeping Room #2* which had neither light nor ventilation and was stifling in its stillness. Pulling on my cold jeans in the dark, all I wanted was some air. I felt my way out into an unlit hallway, then into a cavernous hangar filled with Grumman aircraft in various states of repair. The hangar was still dark, and the smell of aviation fuel and solvents filled the air. The only sounds in the huge room were mine. I was stepping over airplane parts, dodging them in a kind of obstacle course to keep from breaking my ankle or tripping on something in the blackness. The faint outline of a door with thin ribbons of light leaking from its edges led me outside.

The sun was just on its way up, lighting some of the boulders with soft streaks of orange and casting long shadows on the mesquites. I took in a deep gulp of the dawn air, exhaling slowly and casting away my sleeping-room claustrophobia. There was not much around, save for a few gnarled trees that had been victims of Texas's infamous oak wilt. The big hangar I had emerged from specialized in Grumman airplanes and was the only building on the flat horizon for miles. I was here to pick up a Grumman AA-1 and fly it 1,029 miles to its home base in California. It had been here for months undergoing extensive modifications and repairs, and its owner had asked me to fly it back with him. We would be launching this morning.

Standing under that purple sky for several minutes, I was considering the old aviator's adage, "Never fly a just-maintained airplane over a long distance without a place to land," when a crisp November breeze kicked up, interrupted my thought, and prompted me to retreat to the warmer hangar. It was still silent at this hour except for the familiar tick-tack of a big dog walking along the concrete floor, and the muffled sounds of its likely owner.

"Morning! What's your dog's name?" I asked with way too much enthusiasm for the hour.

"Daisy," came the grumbled response from underneath a gray hoodie.

Daisy was a black lab with brown, playful eyes, and paws as big as catcher's mitts. *"Every airport needs a dog like Daisy,"* I thought to myself. There is something soothing about them, with their kind eyes and boundless desire for affection. Dogs radiate calm and are uninterested in the hubris of aviators, so they are the perfect companions. Pilots are drawn to dogs in an almost telepathic way, and our connection to them stretches back to the early days of aviation. German WWI flying ace Manfred von Richthofen (the "Red Baron") would often fly with his beloved dog, Moritz, at his side. And Umberto Nobile piloted the airship Norge over the first North Pole crossing in 1926 with his loyal dog, Titina, right beside him. A dog is to an airport as a horse is to a cattle ranch—essential.

At this sleepy hour, petting Daisy felt like home. I had a German Shepherd of my own and I was missing my loyal friend. I considered that Daisy's entire day would consist of naps, ear-scratches from the mechanics and pilots, and more than a few walks to chase rabbits and relieve herself. My day would be far more complicated. Maybe dogs know something we don't.

From a far corner, I could hear the Grumman's owner, Don, already awake and making conversation. Don was a morning person, and a cheerful one at that. He was the guy that you wanted running your operation—whatever that operation might be—because he got things done on time and with a smile on his face. He was an engineer, a musician, and a skilled carpenter. In his work life he specialized in human prosthetics, so he always had interesting and uplifting stories. Don liked to do things the right way and follow the rules, and people liked him. I'd never seen Don get angry, and he was an optimist at heart. His love of Mexican food, music, and airplanes matched mine, so we got along great.

Don also loved karaoke, which I loathed. He and his wife were serious enough about karaoke that they used the correct Japanese pronunciation of the word ("kadah-OH-keh"), and even threw their own karaoke parties, both of which had become a great source of good-natured ribbing between us, especially in the cockpit. Don was also new to aviation, and I had been his flight instructor from the beginning. He'd been coerced into buying this airplane by a well-meaning pilot friend who probably didn't know the quirky characteristics of the first-generation AA-1.

Don's AA-1 was an early version of the two-seat trainer designed by eccentric aerospace engineer Jim Bede in 1963. Bede would go on to design the famous BD-5 microjet that appeared in the James Bond film Octopussy. He had imagined the AA-1 as a "kit" airplane that pilots would build in their garages using honeycombed aluminum bonded together instead of the more common sheet metal and rivets. It had a long list of odd-but-innovative design elements. Disagreements between Bede and his shareholders led to him being ousted and his company renamed American Aircraft. The new company continued refining the AA-1 until the FAA finally certified the much-modified airplane in 1967 as a factory-built trainer. Aerospace behemoth Grumman bought American Aircraft and continued producing newer, better versions of the AA-1.

This early model was a terrible airplane for new pilots. Pull the nose up a little too much and air burbled over the short, stubby wings, destroying lift and causing a wing to drop without warning into an aerodynamic stall. Neglect rudder control and it would go into a spin, a condition from which the AA-1 could not recover. It landed too fast, and its wing flaps were almost useless. With its stock engine, the airplane was underpowered, carried insufficient payload, and had a fuel range of only ninety minutes. The airplane's "cute" appearance belied the fact that it could kill you without effort.

Back at the hangar, I tried to lure Don outside so we could find his airplane and start the process of getting out of here. We needed to cover a lot of miles today and we still had things to do. Don's bright-blue Grumman was easy to spot out on the ramp, looking like an expectant duckling in the morning light. Giving the airplane a cursory check, I noticed the fuel tanks were already half-empty. That meant we had only 45 minutes before we'd be flying on fumes. The only place to fill up was at Kimble County airport, 30 minutes away, and then nothing for 75 miles after that. So, if there was a problem with the pumps at Kimble, we'd be stranded. It was a problem that would recur at every fuel stop along our route. This was not a cross-country airplane.

I was concerned, because Don's airplane had been heavily modified during its stay here. The long list of new parts and structural enhancements included red-flag items like the wings being removed and re-installed. The internal wing support struts had been replaced with stronger ones to allow the airplane to carry more weight. A new carburetor had been installed, new avionics added, and a new propeller put on to try to improve the Grumman's anemic cruise speed. There were dozens more items. The airplane we were about to fly was not the airplane that had arrived here months ago in that it had been upended mechanically, and that meant there could be unwelcome surprises in store.

With big modifications like the Grumman's, it was customary for the maintenance shop to test-fly the airplane several times before handing it over to its owner. But there had not been time in the days prior, though the mechanics *had* performed one single takeoff and landing. We would be the test pilots on this sortie- a situation I did not like at all.

Looking over the pile of parts the shop had saved and that we had to carry back, I made some calculations. We would be heavy—at our absolute maximum takeoff weight of 1,580 pounds. Because we had to get fuel every ninety minutes, we would always be lifting off at our maximum. The extra weight coupled with an unseasonal heat wave along our route would make each takeoff a challenge, with warm, thin air degrading the engine's already marginal performance and robbing our inadequate wings of precious lift. I sifted through the parts mound, determined to leave behind anything that wasn't essential.

Walking back inside, I could hear the familiar swat of a wooden screen door hitting the frame every time somebody came in or out. Screen doors were popular in Texas, and this one's little shock-absorber had worn out decades ago. The chief mechanic, Stu, had just arrived and made his way toward us. Stu was a fifty-something, no-nonsense guy with a baseball cap and the worldly eyes of a man who had seen and heard everything. In the Grumman world, he was a guru, knowing all the intimate details of making this flying oddity an even better airplane. With his arms full of bags and papers and coffee, he greeted us, then veered off into an office with Don to finish all the paperwork so we could get going.

I had directed Don to do all the flight planning for this trip, and he had been meticulous in putting all the details into a spreadsheet and into an aviation app on his iPad—the modern equivalent of paper sectional charts, plotters, and pencil lines. Our course would take us west near the Mexican border, through most of Texas, then on toward El Paso and beyond. Our plan was to fly as far as our cramped seats and bladders would allow, spend the night about halfway, then continue through New Mexico and Arizona, and on to southern California the next day. There was nothing alarming in the weather forecasts, nor any condition that would cause concern. November was a good time to fly in Texas, and the only worrying element was an astronomical one: the night before had brought the longest lunar eclipse since the fifteenth century, and the final one for a long time. I considered the implications.

Mark Twain had been born and had died during the passing of Halley's Comet in 1835 and 1910, respectively. The assassination of Julius Caesar has been associated with the Great Comet of 44 BC, and the devastating and mysterious Great Chicago Fire of 1871 has been traced to the burning tail of a passing meteor. Central America was rocked by tremendous earthquakes just hours before the first total solar eclipse there since 1918. And we shouldn't forget that Mexico's strongest earthquake in a century—at 8.1 on the Richter scale—hit just after a total eclipse in September of 2017. For us sensitive (or superstitious) souls who believe astronomical events influence earthly matters, the previous night's eclipse was a portentous omen. Resigned to what the fates might bring, I climbed onto the wing and swung my leg over the side and into the AA-1's right seat.

CHAPTER 2

With the paperwork completed and a green light from the mechanics, I began the contortions necessary to secure myself into the Grumman. By now, strapping into an airplane had become second nature, and latching the four-point harnesses on N5917L (this Grumman's registration number) made me feel, once again, like part of the machine. Don followed, and we both took that little breath and long exhale that transitions the mind from ground-dweller to pilot and signals the beginning of a flying adventure. My job was to watch over things and handle the radio, but Don would fly the plane. He had been a little unsure of the Grumman, and my goal was to instill some confidence in him during this long journey.

The big Texas sky beckoned, so we started the engine—which gave off a few reluctant coughs—and let it warm up after its months-long hibernation. At the end of the runway, we did a long, careful runup—the process of bringing an engine to full power and checking everything before takeoff. Pilots do this before every flight to catch a problem before becoming airborne, when there are few options, if any. Checklist completed, engine warmed, and all systems go, I pressed the little black "com" button on the left side of the control wheel (pilots call it a "yoke"), activating the radio transmitter.

"*Silver Wings, traffic, Grumman one-seven Lima departing runway three-five, left-crosswind departure.*"

At airports without a control tower, pilots self-announce their intentions on a common radio frequency. Other pilots in the area will tune to the same frequency so they can form a mental picture of who is doing what and where. Local pilots often acknowledge those radio calls, but this morning there was only static. In sleepy hangars across this part of Texas, pilots would still be warming their hands on their coffee cups, and crop dusters would be filling their hoppers with whatever they needed to spray that day. At this hour we'd be the only airplane in the air for miles, and the radio silence confirmed it.

I watched over Don as he taxied the airplane into takeoff position by aligning it with the center of the runway. He eased the throttle forward and worked the rudder pedals to keep the nose tracking straight as our speed increased. My eyes were now laser focused on the engine gauges to make sure everything looked good before we committed to flying. If we had a problem, the only things that would greet us at the other end of the runway were a huge oak tree and a sturdy fence.

"Forty . . . fifty . . . sixty." I called out the airspeeds as the airplane rolled faster. After a few seconds, Don eased back on the yoke and pointed the Grumman's nose just above the horizon. The wings transformed the metal machine into a bird, and I felt that familiar sigh of the main wheels leaving the ground. The runway disappeared beneath us as we began to fly. It felt as exciting as it had been the very first time I experienced it as a kid. The exhilaration of takeoff had been etched into my—and every pilot's—soul.

The first few moments after takeoff are the most critical in any airplane. The engine is at its limit, and if something breaks, you don't have many options. In the AA-1, there is not enough room to glide until you're about six hundred feet above the ground. You dare not turn back before that because the airplane won't have enough speed or lift, so it'll spin into a smoking hole. Six hundred feet takes over a minute to reach in this airplane, but it feels like a million years. Below us were only sharp boulders and craggy oak-wilt corpses.

Immediately, we had our first problem. I heard the unmistakable buzz of the stall warning—an audible alarm that tells the pilot when airflow over the wings is becoming unstable. It meant we were heavy, the nose was too high, and we were too slow. Leave it like that and we would become intimate friends with the tree trunks and rattlesnakes. "Push the nose down," I told Don in a calm but insistent voice, reverting to flight-instructor mode. Instinctively, my hand moved to the control wheel, ready to push it if Don lagged. We needed to get the nose down and more air flowing over those stubby wings. Don did just that, and in seconds the stall warning went silent. We were back to flying.

Below us the Texas countryside splayed out like an IMAX movie. Far off in the distance, the neat square lines of ranches and roads stretched to the horizon. The higher we went, the more everything looked to be a mottled tan color. That fabled Texas sky was deep blue, becoming richer as we climbed. It was a beautiful morning to fly.

The next hint of trouble came at 4,500 feet.

We'd been flying for twenty minutes when I noticed an odd vibration. It was a faint, intermittent tremor at a frequency that gave it a rhythmic feel, almost like tribal drums at a great distance. I didn't mention it to Don, who was beaming about how smooth the new propeller felt. I surveyed the oil pressure, oil temperature, exhaust gas temperature, and cylinder head temperature gauges, but the only thing I noticed was that our number-three cylinder was running about thirty degrees hotter than the others. I adjusted a few things to see if that made a difference, but the numbers didn't budge. Still, there was no cause for alarm. Number three was a rear cylinder on the engine case. That meant it had less cooling from the oncoming airflow than the cylinders up front. A higher temperature was not unexpected, but I would watch it.

My thousands of hours as a flight instructor had imbued me with a sixth sense when it came to mechanical issues. An instructor had to be ready to take over if a problem occurred so the student wouldn't panic. That meant anticipating engine problems before they became serious. It meant a part of your brain was always monitoring the airplane's systems.

I once had an engine failure on takeoff with a brand-new student. As he began to climb away from the runway, I could sense a hesitation in the engine's power. I reached for the control stick by instinct. Only seconds later the propeller came to a stop just as I had anticipated. But I was so ready that I banked the airplane back to the runway, declared an emergency and landed in the opposite direction without a thought. The student hadn't noticed anything was wrong and surmised it was all part of the lesson. Undaunted, he came back and is a licensed pilot today. Anticipation was my business.

A "Low Fuel" annunciation snatched my attention just as Kimble County Airport came into view. We still had about thirty minutes worth of gas, so the situation wasn't dire, but Kimble was a welcome sight anyway. The radio was still quiet as we banked the airplane to line up on the runway. I could see a few people stirring around the hangars below. My finger went again to the com button.

"Kimble County traffic, low-wing Grumman one-seven Lima turning base to final, runway tree-fife, Kimble."

Non-aviators are often curious about the language pilots use on the radio. Much of it came about because of the dismal radios that were in use in the 1930s and '40s. Headsets had not yet been invented, so pilots would hear radio transmissions through cheap, tinny speakers. Added to the noise of the engines and propellers, radio transmissions got lost in the din, and it became almost impossible to make out words with any accuracy. *Nine* sounded identical to *five,* which sounded the same as the letter *i* or *y*. Certain letter combinations like *th* and words with the letter *v* were almost inaudible. To make communications more reliable, an entire aviation shorthand called the *phonetic alphabet* was created, and some words were changed to sound clearer. *Three* became *tree*, and *five* became *fife*, and *nine* became *niner.* A new language was born. The radios used in airplanes today haven't changed much since WWII, so we still use that unusual lexicon to communicate.

"*Kimble County traffic, one-seven Lima, short final, tree-fife, Kimball.*"

Minutes later, Don made a whisper of a landing and we taxied to the fuel island to top off the tanks. I considered the task ahead. Fueling an aircraft is an involved process where a ground wire is connected to both the pump and the airplane to eliminate sparks and a resulting fire. Mechanisms are heavy and unwieldly, and often don't work due to their constant exposure to harsh weather. For these reasons, fueling the Grumman was a two-person operation. We had accomplished all the required steps and Don pulled the nozzle trigger when a stream of fuel shot out from under the landing gear legs.

"Uhhh!" Don exclaimed, "Where in the heck is *that* coming from?"

Fuel leaking from anywhere was never good, so my heart sank. Turning off the nozzle, Don went in for a closer look with a flashlight and discovered the problem was not insurmountable. The Grumman had a plastic overflow hose on each tank. If someone overfilled the tanks, the excess fuel escaped through the tubes and drained to the ground. The shop had somehow overlooked this tube, which was by now deteriorated and cracked. The high-pressure fuel had shattered it and fuel was leaking out through the wing. We gave the hose a careful cleaning and wrapped it in gummy Flex-Tape, the aviator's secret weapon. It was temporary but effective. We fired the little Lycoming engine back up, taxied out and took off. I watched for any sign of trouble from our quick repair, but it looked fine. Our plan was to refuel again in Fort Stockton and continue to El Paso for lunch. By now we hadn't eaten in twenty hours, and we were starving.

This leg to Fort Stockton would stretch the fuel range of the little Grumman to its limit. If everything went as planned, we would land with about 3 gallons of fuel—maybe twenty minutes' worth. But it would require us to manage the engine with meticulous precision. Our power settings, fuel/air mixture, and speed would need to be more exact than ever. Our wind calculations would have to be correct and unchanging—unlikely in practice. A headwind would eat into our reserve, and if it were strong enough, we wouldn't even make the runway. But there was not another fuel stop anywhere along our way, so up we went. Those matters—and the odd vibration, which had returned—filled my thoughts as the Texas countryside unrolled beneath us like a painted treadmill.

Don and I filled the time with jokes, aviation stories, and all the topics two pilots could conjure up while hurtling through a cloudless blue sky at 110 miles per hour. In between stories, we'd look at our fuel flow meter and watch the number get smaller. When it reached 2.5, our banter went silent. With just over two gallons available, we had only minutes of fuel. There was nothing but cattle country below, with no sign of the Fort Stockton airport. *Come on, runway, where are you?* I thought. I could still feel that rhythmic vibration, and I surmised it was coming from deep inside the engine. There are few feelings more helpless than being in an airplane that is almost out of fuel. The ground that you were admiring just thirty minutes before becomes an adversary in a game of "where can I land without hitting anything?" Even small airplanes need a couple of football fields' worth of space to stop. With my eyes darting around looking for an emergency stretch of road we could land on if the engine quit, I spotted the long runway at Fort Stockton. It loomed like a giant flag. We would make it after all. A huge relief swept over both of us.

CHAPTER 3

Fort Stockton airport sat on the edge of a tiny town that had once been called Comanche Springs. It used to have the largest source of well water in Texas, but it had dried up due to over-farming. Then, when the oil boom hit, the town prospered again from its oil fields, but nearly disappeared during the bust period that followed. It was renamed Fort Stockton and became a bustling pilot training location during WWII, boasting a runway almost two miles long, with four cavernous wooden military hangars that could still be seen for miles. The airport's only draw now was a 24-hour fuel pump with the cheapest- and only- airplane gas for miles.

"*Fort Stockton traffic, Grumman one-seven Lima entering downwind on the 45, runway one-two.*" There was no reply.

Lining up for runway one-two, I saw no sign of human activity. That seemed odd. From our perch at eight hundred feet, there was no evidence of airplanes or people or movement of any kind. The emptiness made me feel uneasy. Still, the now insistent "low fuel" warning had to be sated, so with a light chirp the AA-1 gave up its lift and we taxied off the runway and came to a stop.

"*Fort Stockton, one-seven Lima clear runway one-two. Any local pilots know where the pumps are located?*" No response.

"*Fort Stockton, ahhh, any pilots out there?*"

"*Fort Stockton traffic, radio check . . .*"

It was no use. We were alone. Don pulled out his airport diagram (a good pilot knew to always prepared) and we taxied the thirsty Grumman to where we figured the self-serve pumps might be. We found them at the far south end of the airport, where a lone SUV sat outside one of the big hangars.

"Can you believe there's another human here?" Don laughed as he shut down the engine in front of the pumps. "I was beginning to think Texas had been deserted."

"Well, all I care about is some food right now," I said. "I'm gonna find us both something to eat, if you can handle the pumps on your own?"

"Sure!" Don answered, in a good-natured grin. "Maybe you can find us some Tex-Mex..."

Don began the fuel-pump rigmarole by himself while I searched for the driver of the truck. I figured that big hangar was a good place to start. Because of the bright sun, the inside of the hangar looked black as night. I peered around a corner and, after my eyes had adjusted, saw a man on a ladder. He was wearing a plaid shirt and grey dress slacks and didn't look at all like the cowboys we'd met in Texas so far. For one thing, he had no hat. He reminded me of a school board president. He was focused on repairing something in the eighty-year-old wooden beams that held up what was left of the hangar roof. I called up to him calmly so as not to disturb his precarious footing on that rickety ladder.

"Ahhhh, excuse me. Hi, how ya doin'? Hey, we just landed in that Grumman over there and we're fueling up on the way to El Paso. You wouldn't happen to have any vending machines or know of any food around here, would ya?"

The man looked my way for a second but didn't respond right away. I could tell he was finishing whatever he was doing.

"Mmmm. Well, nothing here really. That old FBO building across the way there just has some furniture in it and a bathroom and the UNICOM radio. The whole thing is getting torn down soon. And these hangars are pretty much empty. Not much going on around here, I'm afraid." He grabbed a dirty rag to wipe his fingers and took another breath to talk.

"I'm the FBO manager."

"FBO" meant "fixed based operator," and the term referred to a facility where pilots and passengers in private airplanes stop enroute to enjoy amenities like full-service fuel, free snacks, rental cars, meeting rooms, and plush resting areas. They're like private airport terminals and are often located at busy airports and posh resort areas frequented by private jets. Fort Stockton seemed like the last place you'd find an FBO.

He must have heard me hold back a laugh, because he gave me a disapproving look and explained that they were moving the FBO to this hangar, anticipating more business. The old building it was housed in had been built in the 1930s. I was perplexed as to why an airport with no airplanes needed an FBO in the first place.

"Do you get much traffic out here?" I asked, emphasizing the word *traffic* while trying not to insult the man. He possessed the neutral calm of, say, an accountant or a funeral director.

"Not really, no."

I expected him to elaborate, but instead he stepped off the ladder, walked in silence to the edge of the hangar door where I was standing, and pointed toward the FBO building, next to which there was another vehicle, hidden by an overhang.

"We had an Uber driver around here 'bout a year ago, but he died," the man related, without a hint of irony. "The keys to that Ford Explorer there are hanging in the service stairway. That's behind a blue door that you can't miss. You can take it into town—just leave the gas full."

The creaky old building looked like a pavilion you'd see on a postcard from the Hamptons or at the end of a sunny pier in California circa 1940. It was low and square with a narrow center section that went up two stories and featured a rotating, high-intensity light beacon on top of a slanted roof. The bright beacon flashed white and green at night and when the weather was poor to signal to aviators that a safe landing spot existed there. The place reminded me of an episode of the *Twilight Zone* where a traveling couple come upon a town with no people. Just like the houses in that episode, this FBO had empty chairs, open magazines on tables, and a half-full coffee cup, but there was nobody in sight. There was only static coming out of the wall speakers that broadcast the Unicom—the radio frequency pilots use to communicate when landing and taking off. That, and the howling winds which were kicking up now, made it all feel abandoned.

We found the keys to the truck behind the blue door, just as the man had said, and took the sand-beaten Explorer to a Tex-Mex place in town called Pepito's. Though the place was deserted, the food was rustic, spicy, and plentiful. We ate enough for four people. Fort Stockton wasn't much of a town, but you could see the remnants of where a thriving place had once been, supporting the throngs of military aviators on their way to war. Now it—like the airport—existed only as a place to get fuel on the way to somewhere else.

When we got back to the airport, the FBO-guy was gone. The hangar was still open though, yawning from the wind now shrieking across its huge doors. It would be best if we got going before the wind and dust became too much for the puny Grumman.

Spurred on by full bellies and fuel tanks, we taxied to the runway and began the choreographed challenge-and-response of the pre-takeoff checklist. We calculated that we had about five more hours of daylight, so we were confident we'd make El Paso before nightfall. Don tucked the completed checklist in between the seats and gave his shoulder harness a final tug while I tuned to the radio frequency for this airport. It was time to go. Everything felt right until Don pushed the throttle forward. At precisely 1,700 RPM on the tachometer, the whole airplane shook and the engine misfired and lost all its power. He tried again but got the same result: the airplane would lurch forward a few inches, the power would fall, and then the engine would almost die in a limp sputter. I took over and attempted the takeoff myself, leaning the mixture control to alter the flow of fuel into the carburetor. But there was no change. I tried switching magnetos—the devices that sent electrical power to the spark plugs—but the attempt yielded the same result: a complete loss of power.

Pilots' minds are trained to go into automatic trouble-shooting mode when there is a problem, so a dozen possible solutions flooded my brain, and I methodically tried each one to no avail. There had to be something I was overlooking. I pulled out the pre-takeoff checklist again and went through each item in plodding detail. I pushed the throttle forward, and the familiar engine cough and loss of power recurred. Nothing I did made any difference. The engine idled OK, but It was clear we couldn't take off.

I blurted out the best expletive I could muster. I don't like swearing, but in this case, I backed it with all the oomph I could manage. We were still sitting at the end of the runway, a mile from the ramp, and the wind was furious now. "Son of a b——"

Our situation was grim. We were in the middle of nowhere. There were no people or maintenance facilities here, and we were almost two hundred miles from any airport that had a mechanic. The ramp had no tie-down chains or ropes, so even a small dose of those famous Texas winds would lift the diminutive Grumman like a dandelion and smash it into a crumpled mess. The "town" had no busses, trains, or even taxis. There were no airplanes on the airfield, which was mostly abandoned. We didn't know what was wrong with the engine, and we didn't have any tools. All of this meant we had no way of getting home—we were stranded.

Adding to our predicament were immovable obligations. We both had jobs to return to with looming deadlines on major projects. We both had companies relying on us being there Monday morning. The Thanksgiving holiday was just days away with its family demands and travel. Don and I had squeezed this trip into a narrow window with no buffer, thinking it would be routine.

We limped the plane back to the ramp with just a trickle of engine power and a helpful tailwind pushing us along the taxiway. Shutting the airplane down, we unlatched the engine cowling—the shroud of aluminum that covered it. Both Don and I traced all the wires, hoses, and linkages in the engine. We went through every system looking for anything that could be a source of trouble. But each prospect led to a dead end. It meant whatever the problem was, it wouldn't be something obvious or something we could repair without a major effort. I was certain the odd vibration I had felt was related to this. Out of ideas, we phoned the shop we had just left that morning, hoping their expertise and familiarity with this airplane would point us toward a plan.

"Hi," Don shouted into his cell phone, the wind blowing so hard it was difficult to hear. "It's Don… yeah, the blue Grumman. Hey, our engine lost power on takeoff and every time we push in the throttle, it dies. We're stuck in Fort Stockton and we can't take off. Can you guys help us?"

"Uh-oh. Well, it could be a lot of things," came the measured response from Stu. "I would start by checking all the connections, hoses, and maybe check the linkages on the . . ."

"We already did all that," Don interrupted, frustrated. "We checked the fuel for water and checked every inch of that engine. It's something more serious." There was silence while Stu conferred with one of his mechanics before responding.

"Well Don, the thing is we're almost eight hours from you if we drove out there," Stu told us. "And without knowing the exact problem, we wouldn't know what parts or tools to bring with us." He had a point. "You'll have to narrow it down more and then we could maybe come out after Thanksgiving . . ."

Stu's admonishment was a hard truth. We were too far away for them to help us, and we didn't know what was wrong in the first place. Don talked to Stu for a few more minutes, but all I heard was a "Good luck!" before he hung up.

I had an ace in the hole. Maybe. It was my good friend Peter, a brilliant aircraft mechanic who shared an airplane with me back home. He was a master at troubleshooting, and we'd spent hours chasing down airplane problems together. Peter answered on the first ring.

"Hey Peter! Man, it's good to hear your voice. Hey, we've got a problem. We're stuck in the middle of nowhere in Texas in Don's Grumman, and we've got an engine here that dies every time we advance the throttle. Hits 1,700 RPM and just loses all its power . . ." I further explained the vibration and the high cylinder head temperatures to him. "We can't take off."

Peter had to be one of the most positive people I'd ever met. He was British and funny and smart, and his irreverent humor matched mine so well that we had laughed enough for several lifetimes. Peter was a joy to be around, and he made any problem seem inconsequential. He had been a musician like me, and he had hung out in Pubs with the likes of Tom Jones and Roger Daltrey back in the day. When it came to airplanes, his mind was like a bloodhound, zeroing in on an engine issue with uncanny accuracy.

I could tell by the long silence that Peter's mechanic mind was clicking into gear. He knew this Grumman and had flown it with me before. He took me through a hundred things over the phone, all starting with the phrase, "OK, have you checked . . ." But nothing panned out. We HAD checked everything. The usual suspects were not the cause of this problem. With everything else exhausted, and with the specter of the tribal-drum vibration earlier, Peter and I concluded that we had a major engine issue on our hands—probably a bad cylinder. Given that's where the piston lives and provides all the engine's power, we were in trouble.

To make things worse, Don and I had packed light, knowing we'd be too heavy to fly otherwise. We each had only the proverbial toothbrush and one change of clothes, and we were not prepared for an extended stay. Even if we could have found some way to get home, it would have been a long time before we could locate and contract a mechanic to come to Fort Stockton with tools, order all the correct parts, and meet them for the repair. We couldn't abandon the plane on an unprotected ramp in gale-force winds.

A sudden gust nearly lifted the airplane off the ground. I motioned for Don to help me get the engine cowling back on so it wouldn't blow away and get smashed. The wind was fierce by now, and a brown dust cloud the size of several buildings swirled toward us. We each held the cowling down with both hands and turned our heads away from the blast. Don was shouting something to me, but the roar carried it off as we anchored ourselves onto the airplane with everything we had. Squinting through the gale, I caught a glimpse of what I thought was someone emerging from out of the cloud.

It was a man, and he was dressed in dark pants and a dark long-sleeved shirt. I could make out a red baseball cap on his head with a small emblem of some sort., which he held against the wind with both hands. He moved toward us slowly, approaching like a cautious wolf.

"You boys having some problems?" he yelled over the din.

The question hung in the air as I formulated an answer. The man looked to be in his seventies, with skin like a lawyer's satchel, and he spoke in a gentle sing-song voice with an accent that was familiar. I couldn't formulate where he had come from since we hadn't seen another human since we'd landed and there were no vehicles anywhere except for a yellow earthmover a hundred yards away. I figured he was some airport guy who liked airplanes and just wanted to know what we were doing here in in the middle of a Texas dust storm.

"Yeah, we're having engine problems," I shouted.

He didn't say anything, so I kept going. "We're on our way to California, and this thing loses power every time we push the throttle in, and we've tried everything. We can't take off and we can't stay here, and we have no tools. So, we're trying to figure out what to do."

Again, he didn't respond. I wasn't sure he'd heard me because he looked off toward the highway.

"Well, you might have to hitchhike to El Paso and get a flight from there," he offered at last. "Not much around here." By now the wind and dust had calmed just enough that I could hear and see him clearly. He looked to be an American Indian, and he spoke in the rhythm of a tribal language. Neat, white sideburns jutted out from underneath his hat, and he had an angular, proud face. In an old western he would have been cast as the Indian chief. His eyes were keen and piercing, like a bird of prey. He reminded me of Ricardo Montalbán. "Well, then I guess that's our only option." I felt resigned, having never hitchhiked in my life. The prospect of two middle-aged men getting picked up along an interstate in rural Texas seemed as remote as it did insane. The banjo tune from *Deliverance* came to mind. "What we need is a mechanic, but I'm sure that's the last thing we'll find around here," I finished.

The old man put his weathered hand on the propeller and asked, "Is your ignition off?" I nodded, holding up the key, so he rotated the propeller roughly 180 degrees until you could hear the loud click of the impulse coupler, the spring-loaded mechanism that fires off a spark to the engine when you first start it.

"*I'm* a mechanic," he said, without looking up.

I stared at him, trying to speak just one of the hundred thoughts that came to my mind that instant. I was sure he meant a *truck* mechanic. Maintenance facilities for big rigs were common along Interstate 10. After all, the highway stretches from California to Florida and is filled with freight trucks 24/7. While his was a kind thought, airplanes can only be repaired by those with specialized training. A major repair like this would have to be signed off by an aircraft mechanic with an Inspection Authorization certification, the highest maintenance credential available from the Federal Aviation Administration. If a truck mechanic made a repair on our airplane and we crashed later, no insurance would cover us, and we would be in violation of several federal laws and could be sent to prison. And that's if we survived the crash.

"Wow, that's amazing that you're a mechanic," I told him kindly, "but airplanes can only be worked on by special—"

"No, I'm an *aircraft* mechanic," he interrupted. "I was a crew chief and flew UH-1 Hueys in Vietnam, and I came back here after the war and started my own maintenance shop. Been here ever since."

Don and I looked at each other with obvious suspicion as this odd old man inched his ear closer to the engine and continued to turn the propeller. He swung it all the way around several times before saying anything more. I couldn't tell if he was crazy or concentrating.

"You hear that click?" he finally asked, stopping with one blade in his hand.

"I don't hear anything," I answered, humoring him. I had decided he was crazy.

"That's right. I don't either. You have a bad valve in that number-three cylinder. It might just be sticking, but that's causing your power loss. I'll bet it's running hotter than the others . . ."

At that moment it was as if the Mormon Tabernacle Choir had just finished the big refrain from Handel's "Hallelujah" Chorus. This stranger had spoken secret words that only a real aircraft mechanic would know. And yes, number three *had* been running hot. His hunch could explain our symptoms.

"Why don't you boys push this over there by those doors," instructed the old man.

Fear, frustration, and anger all live in the same place, and by now I was weary from carrying them. The day had gotten away from us, and nightfall was now just hours away. The unnerving emptiness of this place, coupled with the prospect of getting stranded here, left me open to anything this newfound friend suggested.

Don and I pushed the little Grumman toward the two weathered doors. They were part of a smaller structure attached to the side of one of the big military hangars. The windows on this section were yellowed and opaque from the relentless sun, and every pane was broken and covered in spider webs. Weathered plywood had been nailed across some of the openings, and the air smelled of snakes and buzzed with cicadas and hornets.

I didn't know what this man was getting at, but as we rolled the airplane up to the doors, he fiddled with some keys and pushed one of the wide planks of wood to one side. We hadn't asked his name, but with his Native American heritage and his Vietnam history, I started referring to him as, "Chief" – a moniker he approved of with a beaming smile. "Well, that sure does fit me," he laughed.

The Chief turned on the lights and out of the dark appeared the most incredible shop I had ever seen. Brilliant fluorescent lights flooded the hangar with clean, white light. There were air compressors, Snap-on rollaway tool carts, jigs, parts cleaners, wrenches, and every kind of diagnostic tool imaginable. He had an old spark plug tester that was right out of the 1950's but looked new. In the corner was a cabinet full of vacuum tubes from the 1960's. The place had that familiar, heady smell of grease, rubber, avgas, and time.

The old mechanic stepped inside and moved with purpose, gathering tools and turning on switches. It was obvious this place was as familiar to him as his own face in the mirror.

"Let's start by checking the compressions," he announced.

I watched as he worked. He was of medium stature. The red cap he wore was adorned with the head of an eagle and a

Vietnam Army unit with some text. I couldn't make out the writing. His navy-blue shirt was uniform crisp, with hard creases ironed into the long sleeves and breast pockets. He wore a royal-blue ascot, an odd accessory worn mostly by fighter pilots in Vietnam, and he was meticulous in his grooming. He seemed an anachronism.

"They call me the Grouch," he related, talking to us as he removed spark plugs and cooling baffles like a master. "Some people say I'm always in a bad mood." He laughed. "I came here from Mexico when I was little. From the Tepehuán tribe. Then I went to Vietnam and Hueys."

Don was holding the gauges displaying the compression numbers as the chief checked them one by one and called out the results. He paused on the number-three cylinder. "Ah-ha. You got nothing here, see that?" The needle rested near zero. It *was* a bad cylinder. It turns out we had a damaged valve which had been contributing to that vibration. I reached for the phone in my back pocket to begin the process of ordering a replacement cylinder, which, with any luck, would take at least three days to arrive. The chief saw me and held up both hands.

"No, no. I have one here," he said. "I have everything we need right here."

The Lycoming O-320 engine had multiple variants. It was unlikely that this remote outpost in Texas would have the exact parts we needed. Still, we trusted this man—we had no other choice.

The chief's copper-colored hands moved with studied grace as he worked. As promised, he *did* have all the specialized gaskets, nuts, and springs to repair that engine. Don and I assisted by fetching tools, cleaning up, and keeping the parts organized as time passed without notice.

After a little while, the old man suggested we take a break. It was still warm out, but the sun was low on the horizon and the day would soon be over. In Texas, November days are short, and night comes on without much notice.

"Hey, do you boys want to see something?" he asked. By that time Don and I were ready for anything.

"Sure," we answered together, giving each other a quizzical look and wondering what this stranger had up his sleeve.

We followed him toward the far wooden hangar. It was another one of the huge military structures, but its doors were closed. The ramp was so quiet I could hear the loose asphalt crunching under my shoes, and we hadn't seen an airplane land or take off all day. The chief didn't speak but reached into his pocket as we walked, fiddling with his keys again. I noticed he had on worn, black cowboy boots. We stopped in front of two huge doors that had faded from white to a sort of gray color in the unrelenting sun. Each one was two or three stories high. He put a key into a tarnished Master Lock and yanked the clasp open with a loud clunk that echoed inside the cavernous hangar. Late afternoon light streamed in from dirty windows along one side of the hangar and through cracks between the wooden beams all around. Inside were two neat rows of small airplanes. There were maybe fifteen in all. Each was old, with the newest one being a Cessna 177 Cardinal from the mid-1970s. None looked like they had flown in years.

"These are mine," the chief declared with a wave of his hand. "I manage these, and I also fly them."

There were some jewels among the derelict airframes. An intact Piper Tri-Pacer, or as some call it, the "flying three-legged milk stool," stood among the cobwebs. A beautiful Piper Apache twin; a Luscombe and a Taylorcraft; an old Schweitzer glider. They were like museum pieces that had been untouched for decades. I felt like the archaeologists who discovered Egyptian tombs. My eyes came to rest on an Ercoupe with a distinct, sixties-era paint job.

The Ercoupe was a true aviation oddity. It was a two-place airplane first envisioned by aeronautical engineer Fred Weick in 1931 that began production in 1937 under a company called Engineering and Research Corporation (ERCO). The light plane's chief distinction was that it didn't have rudder pedals and was supposed to be spin-proof. A spin is an aeronautical anomaly where the wings lose lift while also being yawed to one side. The result is the airplane plunges downward in a corkscrew manner, and sometimes won't recover.

The Ercoupe came along as an "everyman" airplane that was so easy to fly, every American would have one in their garage, and we'd all be commuting to and from grandma's house in one. A completely new category of pilot's license was created by the Civil Aeronautics Administration for Ercoupe pilots who had never used rudder pedals. But

WWII intervened and took up supplies of badly needed aluminum, and the Ercoupe languished. After the war, despite heavy advertising through Macy's department stores, the Ercoupe failed to hit the sales numbers the company had envisioned. Today they are odd rarities. The airframe that sat before me would have been scooped up by collectors long ago if they knew it existed.

"Yeah, that old Ercoupe got really beat up by hail," the old mechanic remarked, noticing my gaze. "Now we call it 'the golf ball.'" Indeed, the entire airframe was covered in tiny divots from hail, though the plexiglass canopy looked untouched.

But I don't understand," I said. "You own these, or do you fly them for the owners?"

"Well. I fly them whenever I want. The owners like to keep 'em flying, so I take them out sometimes. I sort of inherited them, but I don't have room for any more. I just have too many airplanes."

We were learning more about this stranger. This man was a licensed pilot. Even though I hadn't understood his arrangement with these flying machines, I was fascinated by each one and by the fact that he flew them all. That hangar was every airplane-nerd's dream. What I didn't understand was why they all looked so neglected if the chief flew them.

We continued walking through the hangar when the old man pointed out an odd-looking, high-winged airplane that looked like a homemade toy, sitting in a far corner. It was made of aluminum tubing covered with nylon or polyester fabric. I had never seen whatever this flying machine was, and it was covered in thick dust, with weeds growing high under each flat tire. The fuselage was crumbled. I could see a beehive or wasp's nest inside the cabin, and I could make out one half of the faded word "EXPERIMENTAL" beneath a layer of dirt. This was a homemade design of some sort, and it had been severely damaged at some point decades ago. Looking it over, I wouldn't have strapped myself into that thing for all the gold in California.

The chief spoke up. "I crashed in this..."

His words stayed in the air like mine had out on the windy ramp. I was filled with questions and expected he would tell us more, but his long pause left us wondering.

"Yeah, I was trying to land, and the controls got stuck," he shared. "It was pretty bad..." He didn't seem to want to say much more, so Don and I just gave each other a perplexed look while the old man surveyed his hangar in silence. "Yeah, so these are my little projects. I'll be working on them forever I suppose . . ."

As we walked toward the opposite set of wooden doors, I noticed a curious thing: the hangar floor was above the concrete airport ramp. At some point, the concrete apron that led into the hangar had been demolished. It left an eight-foot-high gap between the ramp and the floor of the hangar. In other words, there was no way to taxi these airplanes out. You couldn't roll them from the hangar to the taxiway because of the drop at each end. They would have to be removed with a crane.

"Wait a minute. The floor of this hangar is . . ." I started,

"Well, we better head back and get your airplane fixed," interrupted the old man. "We don't have much daylight left."

The three of us walked back to the shop without talking. We were tired and I was still marveling at the luck we'd had in finding an airplane mechanic at this abandoned airfield. With several hours gone and the sun now touching the horizon, the chief turned a few more wrenches on the engine, reassembled everything, and told us he would run a final compression check on each cylinder. He handed Don the compression gauges and went to each cylinder, turning the propeller to build pressure, then read the number off the gauge as if announcing the results of a horse race. Eighty PSI was the target, and each one was right on the money. I could see the satisfaction in his sly smile as he checked each cylinder, not even paying much attention to the numbers. He knew his work was more than good.

"We're all done! But now somebody needs to test this thing," he proclaimed with a swipe of his red shop rag.

CHAPTER 4

Testing an airplane after a major repair was a delicate business. A forgotten wrench, a loose nut, an incorrectly tightened screw—anything could have brought the entire thing down. "I'll take her up," I conceded, though that was obvious. I was the only choice for test pilot, since Don was too inexperienced.

The sky had turned a dark, aquamarine blue and the late fall temperature had dropped. I knew the cold would give my wings extra lift, and I'd be light anyway since I had jettisoned everything out of the plane earlier. The sun sitting below the horizon provided just enough light that I could see the whole runway. I strapped in and yelled the customary "Clear!" and pushed the START button on the instrument panel.

The engine came to life in just two turns of the propeller and expelled a little puff of triumphant white smoke. The O-320 felt as smooth as ever as I studied the gauges. Everything looked good, so I taxied the little bird to the end of the longest runway available.

At 7,500 feet long, runway one-two would give me the best chance of survival if the engine quit on takeoff. I could put the plane down before meeting the power lines and trees at the far end. The windsock showed a strong crosswind from my right, so I'd have to deal with that.

With my heart pounding and a little prayer still caught in my throat, I advanced the throttle and watched the RPM gauge: 1,500 . . . 1,600 . . . moment of truth . . . 1,700 . . . then 1,800. The motor felt strong and hummed along at a frequency that was solid and reassuring. The Grumman was rolling fast— the tachometer read 2,450 RPM now, and she leapt off the runway like the clichéd homesick angel.

OK, concentrate on the airplane.

Airspeed was right at ninety. Vertical speed was eight hundred feet per minute. Every gauge on the panel was in the green. Reaching six hundred feet above the ground, I gingerly banked the AA-1 to the left and continued my climb. I'd only go up another four hundred feet, stay at that altitude, then make a pass along the runway. Below I could make out the faint figures of Don and the old man standing along the taxiway.

The engine was running better than ever as I made that first cautious pass. It was perfect. I was so elated that I followed it with a second "airshow pass" where I zoomed down to just five feet above the runway at high speed and pulled the Grumman up into a graceful climbing arc. It's what airshow pilots do to wow the crowd. The airplane felt brand new.

The great Charles "Chuck" Yeager – the first pilot to break the speed of sound in an airplane- attributed the success of his flying career to the fact that he was scared a lot of the time. He made it a point to know every screw, every wire, and every system on his airplanes. He knew the systems better than the mechanics themselves. It was this mechanical knowledge coupled with his healthy respect for safety that allowed him to keep flying into his nineties. I was thinking about this as I wiped my sweaty hands on my shirt and craned my ear to hear the slightest hesitation in the engine. But there was none. This was a healthy airplane, and I knew it and felt it in all my pilot senses. Now I could relax a little bit.

I made one last, uneventful pass along the flightline to prove to all of us that we had a working airplane, then rolled the AA-1 back onto the weather-beaten runway without a snag. I taxied it back to the shop with my canopy pushed open, like a movie fighter pilot. Night had arrived, so we couldn't set out for El Paso until early the next morning, but it felt like we'd just won the lottery.

The chief and Don were beaming as I shut the engine down in front of them. "It ran *perfectly*," I offered without hesitation. The chief smiled. Don spoke to him first as I finished turning off switches. "I…WE don't even know what to say or how to thank you for helping us," he began, reaching for his wallet, "but whatever you want to charge us is OK with me. You saved us in more ways than you'll ever know, and I'd like to pay you right now."

"Put your wallet away," growled the old man, his brow furrowing. "I don't want your money. I do this because I like to help pilots in trouble."

I interrupted. "Well, we're hugely grateful for that. Believe me. But your parts and all the hours you spent with us—they aren't free," I countered. "It wouldn't be fair if we didn't pay you. We'd be taking advantage of you."

"No. I really don't need money anymore," he said, which I thought was an odd comment. A man of his age couldn't be working full time, and he didn't seem to be wealthy. But his voice held a defiant stir. It was clear he was ending this conversation. The chief removed his cap, revealing perfectly white hair, then replaced it for effect.

"OK. You win," I said, holding up both hands and figuring I'd try to pay him again the next day. "But we just want you to know how grateful we are and how miraculous it was for you to be here today. I still can't believe our luck. In fact, I've been meaning to ask you, how did—"

"We have to get you boys where you can get some food and some sleep," the old man interrupted, and he turned off the lights and closed the big doors.

I had so many questions for this mysterious man, but I was exhausted to the point of collapse. The elation of the test flight, the stress of the day, the pre-dawn alarm clocks, and the mental fatigue of working through our problems had taken their toll. I was drained and hungry. Don looked just as spent. The chief sensed it.

"Why don't one of you taxi your airplane over to the far hangar and we'll just push it in there for the night," he suggested. "I know the airport manager, and he won't mind if you take the loaner car. There'll be someplace in town you can stay."

We all agreed, so I started the plane back up and taxied alone to the hangar where I had met the FBO guy that morning. By now, night had fully descended on the airport, and it felt like a lone outpost on a desolate planet. Standing in front of the dark hangar, it was so quiet I could hear my own heartbeat. I waited outside for Don and the chief, who drove up in a 1971 Ford pickup.

Don and I pushed the Grumman into a corner of the hangar and walked back out. As I glanced over my shoulder, the AA-1 looked a little lost and scared in the vast darkness of that creaky old building. I had always believed that airplanes had souls, and this one seemed frightened.

"Will you be here in the morning in case we have a problem?" I asked the chief.

"I will," he answered, his arm resting on the door sill and his red cap sitting low. "We fly at dawn."

With that he gave a little salute and drove off into the night. Don and I walked toward the old terminal to retrieve the keys to the loaner truck.

"Oh my gosh!" Don exclaimed. "We never got his name."

With all the distractions, we had not asked the chief about anything beyond the task at hand. We hadn't gotten a business card or a phone number. We didn't know this man's name or the name of his business. We didn't have anything to put into the airplane's maintenance logbook, which is a history of its repair record, with every maintenance item logged in meticulous legal detail. We needed his signoff to fly.

But at that moment, we gave it little thought. By now, the lure of food and rest had taken over our thinking as we walked the two hundred yards toward the old FBO. The ramp was in complete darkness now, with only a faint orange glow in the distance from the illuminated windsock, and I shivered against the cold.

Something caught my eye.

"Hey, what is *that*?"

It was so dark that the stars were the only illumination, but I could make out the faint outline of a shiny, low-wing airplane sitting far out on the ramp. There was no moon, but I could see it had a unique profile. It looked to be a Fairchild PT-19, a World War II trainer and the very airplane type that had been based at this field in the 1940s. What a crazy coincidence. But we hadn't heard any planes all day. No pilot could have slipped into this abandoned airport without making any noise.

We continued toward the building and as we got closer, we could hear the low, muffled sounds of conversation behind closed doors. There were two distinct voices, and it sounded like an instructor and his student. This was a strange time and place for a flying lesson though, especially in a seventy-five-year-old warbird at night. They had likely been on a cross country flight and it got dark, so they set down here. Maybe they needed a ride into town?

I pushed open the wooden door, ready to ask these two where they'd come from, when . . . nothing. There was nobody there, and there were no voices. Behind that door lay nothing but the empty FBO. *But they were here a second ago,* I thought. It was silent except for the radio static. But we *had* heard voices, we were sure of it. The exchange between an instructor and a student was unmistakable and I'd had conversations like it a thousand times. I hunted for any possible explanation and gave Don a scowl. Was it possible they had gone to grab the truck keys?

I flung open the door to the service stairway, but it was dark and still. The keys hadn't budged from where I'd placed them that morning. Ducking my head back out of the stairway, I headed toward the observation room. It was a half-moon-shaped area at the front of the FBO building with an array of paned windows that went up to the ceiling in a 180-arc. It offered a panoramic view of the entire ramp and runway. Maybe the instructor was going over the aeronautical chart with his student before heading back home. But the observation room and the ramp were empty against the black fabric of night, and there were no pilots walking toward their airplane. I could see that the PT-19 itself was also gone—or maybe had never been there. There was nothing but darkness and the limp static of the Unicom. It felt strange in there, as if the air had been sucked out.

Were we just tired? Could the two of us have imagined it? Was it some errant illusion or cosmic, existential debris from that eclipse? Whatever had just happened, I couldn't explain it.

"Let's get out of here," I suggested.

We took the truck again and managed to find a place in town to spend the night, where I took the most glorious hot shower ever. We ate, then retreated to our rooms and I collapsed into the sleep of the dead until that blasted alarm stole it once again.

Driving back to the airport before dawn, it was still dark. We pushed the cold-soaked Grumman out of the eerie hangar and topped off its fuel tanks at the pumps. We would wait until the old man arrived to sign the maintenance logbooks, exchange phone numbers, and we'd try again to pay him for all his work. He'd be here any minute.

But an hour came and went as the lavender light in the east blossomed into a full sunrise. Then two hours. Because yesterday had been wasted, we'd have to make it to California in a single, brutal day of flying. Weather reports were forecasting low visibilities and instrument conditions for southern California by 6 p.m. We needed to get going.

"Let's walk over to his hangar," Don suggested. "Maybe he's asleep in there."

We approached his place and noted a curious thing: the doors looked like they had never been opened. The locks were tarnished and rusty. Odder still, there were waist-tall weeds in front of the doors, and weeds in front of his shop. I hadn't remembered those.

With broken glass crunching everywhere I stepped, I tried to peek into the crack between the doors. I cupped both of my hands around my eyes and peered hard into the dark. I couldn't see a thing.

Were we at the wrong hangar? No. I spotted the fresh stain where oil had spilled from the valve cover yesterday. We had been here before. There were a hundred reasons why the chief hadn't made it that morning, but something seemed off, and both Don and I felt the need to leave. "Look," I offered. "The engine is working fine, and if we don't leave now, we'll never get home in time. We can find this guy another day and square up." We walked back and fired up the AA-1 without comment or ceremony and rolled onto the runway as we completed the takeoff checklist one more time.

Don pushed the throttle forward, and our engine gleefully passed 2,400 RPM. The Grumman's wings took big bites of the thick morning air, and we were airborne in seconds. I knew we were both thinking about the old man and the voices and the hangars and all the unanswered questions we had, but we were relieved that this place had granted us a reprieve of sorts, and that we were—at last—climbing away and headed home.

At six hundred feet I craned my neck back toward the ramp. There was no sign of the chief, nor his truck. Nothing moved. There were no car lights on the horizon. It was as if that airport had been an oasis in a desert of time.

We climbed to 8,500 feet to cross the Guadalupe Pass and let the distance and time pass beneath our wings. The towns slid under us in a succession of blurs, with names like

Lordsburg, Saragosa, and Culberson, each offering the possibility of a runway and a gas pump. Our little blue Grumman ran like a champ the entire way. In the cargo hold we discovered a small bottle of oil additive made especially for Lycoming engines that would keep the valves from sticking on our long trek home. The chief must have slipped it there at some point, knowing we'd find it. Curious luck continued to follow us.

El Paso was a welcome sight with its airliners and massive runways. We thought it a good omen when we saw the famous NASA "Super Guppy" airplane parked on the ramp, it's bulbous aluminum skin gleaming in the sun and looking like a happy cartoon. It's an airplane that makes everyone who sees it smile. We became fueling experts at all the little airports along the way. We even managed to wrestle some potato chips from a cantankerous vending machine at a desert outpost whose name we never got, though it had fuel and working restrooms. Its runway was short and narrow, and confronted us with a stiff crosswind that felt like a furnace blast in the unseasonal heat. I decided to make that takeoff since there was no margin for error. But the little airplane came up to speed just in time to clear the old shack at the far end of the runway, and up we went without issue.

We made it to our refueling stop in Blythe, California in forty-nine minutes, although our flight computer had said it would take seventy. That was critical, because Blythe's fuel pumps closed precisely at 4 p.m. and had no attendant or self-serve option after that. If we missed the cutoff, we'd have to stay overnight and refuel in the morning. With time running short we found the airport and prepared to make our customary rectangular pattern around the field to land. That landing pattern is standard but takes several minutes to complete because part of it takes you *away* from the airport. From our position just east of the runway, a straight-in approach would save precious minutes since we were already aligned for landing. But a straight-in approach at a non-towered airport is frowned upon and can be dangerous. So, in the interest of safety and resigned to being late, I self-announced our standard rectangle pattern entry on the radio. A crisp, professional- and unexpected - voice replied.

"One-seven Lima, this is Blythe tower; can you accept a straight-in, runway two-six? Wind is calm."

The thing was, Blythe Airport didn't have a control tower.

"Blythe tower, one-seven Lima. Ahhh, we can accept that—affirm."

"Roger, one-seven Lima. We have a temporary military tower at Blythe today, in case you're wondering. Cleared to land, two-six."

"Cleared to land, two-six!" I replied.

We made it to the fuel pumps with just two minutes to spare and we finished our fueling without delay. The US Army had installed a temporary control tower at Blythe that day to direct military aircraft taking part in an exercise utilizing the airport. The straight-in landing had saved us from an overnight stay and complex logistics. Fate had intervened once again.

On our final, weary leg home, weather reports showed heavy fog and instrument-only conditions at our airport. Worse still, the fog spread all over the Los Angeles basin and stretched all the way to the Banning Pass, gateway to the desert. This simple reality meant we couldn't land. Don's AA-1 was not equipped with the advanced avionics required to make an instrument-only approach. So, suspended between the featureless desert and the void of a moonless sky, we had to find a place—once again—to spend the night with all the accompanying complications and delays. It was the same old story. As we ran out of options, our radio lit up with an updated weather report.

"Attention all aircraft," came the voice from Los Angeles Center, *"John Wayne ATIS information Delta is current. Forty-five hundred broken, visibility four; altimeter two niner eight seven."*

In aviation-speak, that report reflected the latest weather at our destination, which showed we could make it to the runway without any special instrument procedures or equipment after all. Somehow, that persistent fog at John Wayne Airport had lifted just enough to make it legal for us to land. Elated, we headed straight toward the airport and saw those two big, beautiful, lit-up runways from miles out. My good friend, Nick, who works in the tower at John Wayne, cleared us to land on runway two-zero right, with an added, "Welcome home!" Then, just fifteen minutes after we touched down, the fog rolled back and the airport was, once again, socked in. Drained, bleary-eyed, but relieved, we secured the Grumman one last time and said terse goodbyes while the instrument gyros whirred down. I could hear the airplane's steel exhaust pipe clicking as it contracted in the cool night air, marking the end of our 1,029-mile journey.

CHAPTER 5

In the days that followed, any free time I had I focused on finding the chief. There were so many questions that remained unanswered. Who was he? Where had he come from? How does a maintenance business survive at an airport that is all but deserted? I knew there had to be a way to locate him, and with so much grandiose technology at my fingertips, I felt frustrated that I had not uncovered anything useful. All my leads had been dead ends and I felt defeated, when I finally got through to the Fort Stockton airport manager just days before Christmas.

"Hello. I was just at your airport for a couple of days with engine problems," I explained. "A mechanic there really helped us out and got us home. He was a Native American man—an older guy—and he had been in Vietnam as a Huey crew chief. He owns that amazing maintenance shop there next to the big middle hangar. I was wondering if you could give me his contact information so I can thank him?"

There was a long pause.

"You're looking for *who*?"

I described the mechanic again and added, "He wears a blue ascot."

"I'm sorry, but I think you have the wrong airport. This is Fort Stockton. We do have four military hangars here, but they're mostly empty, and we don't have any mechanic on the field," he said, in a perplexed tone. "We haven't had a mechanic on the field in a while."

"But he's based there," I insisted. "He said he'd been there for a long time."

"I'm sorry but I just don't know anybody like that," the manager told me. "The only person who's around the airport regularly is Ed, the FBO manager. But nobody like you're describing. I'm thinking you just have your airports confused. I'm really sorry."

"I don't think so," I responded, a bit dejected. "But, thanks and good night." I hung up the phone knowing I had the right airport. It didn't make sense that the airport manager didn't know one of his tenants. Disheartened, my thoughts turned to finding the PT-19 and its pilots, who had disappeared into that night. If they were local—and they had to be, landing in Fort Stockton at night—they might know about the old man.

But FAA ownership records showed no airworthy PT-19's registered anywhere near Fort Stockton. Even more perplexing, a search of online flight tracker data showed no trace of a PT-19 flight to Fort Stockton that night—or, in fact, of any other airplane into that airport. A further search by aircraft type showed there were no PT-19s flying on that date, period.

Days passed, but there was still no trace of the chief. Like a bloodhound on the scent, I continued my hunt undeterred. I scoured search engines for anything I could find about Fort Stockton Airport. On the night before Christmas Eve, I made a fascinating discovery: an online archive of military documents from the Fort Stockton area contained a cache of "yearbooks" from the US Army Air Force's 309th Flying Training Detachment at Gibbs Field, which was the original name of the Fort Stockton Airport. Gibbs had been one of many training bases across the country during World War II that took civilian cadets and gave them military flight training.

The commemorative books were awarded to each graduating class up until the unit closed in 1944. Each held the names and photographs of that group of pilots, along with images of their daily lives on base and their flying experiences.

Looking through the photographs of those smiling cadets earning their wings, I imagined their lives so long ago. I had been inside those same buildings where they had been and walked through those same wooden hangars that once buzzed with mechanics and airplanes, eighty years separating us. I had walked the same ramp, and even landed on the same runway that those trainees had bounced and swerved on decades before. That old FBO building absorbed the hopes and dreams of every one of those men.

The boys in those photographs would be at war soon, piloting aircraft in the worst aerial conflict the world had yet seen. They would experience horrors beyond their understanding and would come to know heroism, triumph, and courage. Many of them would never come home. Their legacy still hung in the air at Fort Stockton.

Late that night, browsing through one of the books, a particular page stopped me.

In the yearbook for Cadet Class 44G, a simple tribute on page eighty described a tragedy. On February 4, 1944, Flight Instructor C.R. Fasanella and his student, Billy K. Ferguson, were killed while attempting a night landing at Fort Stockton. Their plane, which had been a Fairchild PT-19, was destroyed. I reread the passage several times, considering the curious coincidence. Just then, my phone rang with a number I didn't recognize.

"Hi! Ah, sorry to bother you this close to Christmas," the voice on the other end said. "I'm Emmett Martin and I know the airport manager at Fort Stockton. I used to work there years ago. He told me you were looking for information on a mechanic there, and I think I may have found something for you."

I was elated that one of my leads had paid off. "Wow," I replied, "you have no idea how good that is to hear! What did you find?"

"Well, he was around back in the seventies and eighties," Emmett relayed. "He was a crew chief on Hueys in Vietnam and had a shop next to the big hangar there after the war. They said he was popular with pilots—they all loved him—and he helped a lotta guys whose airplanes broke down on their way across Texas. After the war, guys with Hueys would bring them to Fort Stockton for maintenance because they trusted him. He was originally from some Indian tribe."

That had to be him.

"He died in a plane crash back in the early nineties," Emmett said. "Didn't say how, but it was a small airplane. I couldn't find the NTSB report, so I don't know what happened exactly. But I did find some notes about him in the files we moved out of the old FBO building. They're tearing it down, you know."

"Yeah, I know," I said. "But wait. You said he died—are you sure? How can that be?"

"Yeah, in a crash at the airport in some little plane," Emmett confirmed. "Did you know him back then?"

"Nah. I just thought I, I had uh, that I had seen him, but then, umm . . . Well, I guess I was wrong."

Emmett laughed. "Yeah, couldn't have been him—he's been gone a long time. Can I ask you why you were looking for him?"

"Well, he helped me and another pilot out . . . I mean, I thought he . . ." I stammered as I searched for the right words. "What I mean is I heard about this mechanic, and he helped a friend . . . ah, it's kind of complicated. Probably a wild goose chase."

"Yeah. OK, well I hope I helped," Emmett finished.

"You did," I answered. "And hey, this is gonna sound strange," I added with much hesitation, "but has anybody ever seen . . . ahhh . . ..Nah, never mind. Merry Christmas." And with that I hung up the phone. The Christmas tree lights twinkled their soft, colored glow as Bing crooned about a white Christmas in the background. I stared at the ground and considered what Emmett Martin had just told me.

Searching for any explanation as to how a dead man could have helped two ill-equipped pilots and their hobbled airplane, I thought about the long-rumored private association that exists among a special group of pilots. It is unofficial and spoken of only in the most remote corners of aviation. There are no dues or membership cards or titles. There is no admittance process, and membership is conferred by chance and without notice. Most aviators don't even know it exists, but I knew because of things I had seen.

On rare occasions, when a group of pilots had gathered in a hangar or briefing room or banquet hall somewhere, an odd ritual would take place. When all the non-fliers had gone and only pilots were left, one of them would stand up and close the doors, as if the words that were about to be spoken were sacred. They'd start with something like, "What I'm about to tell you might sound impossible, but . . ." The others would end their conversations and look down in church-like reverence, without skepticism or argument. They'd hold their cups of coffee or spirits with both hands, as if to protect the moment, and they would nod in silent understanding as each word was spoken.

Each would tell stories of airplanes shot up by war and wounded beyond the ability of staying airborne but somehow bringing their crews back home without explanation; stories of being caught in fog at night over an ocean, lost and low on fuel, and being brought to safety by a disappearing airplane. Another pilot would stand and tell the story of a huge storm vanishing in the instant before almost tearing a jetliner's wings off; of landing fields materializing in jungles and deserts; of fuel tanks enduring far past empty; of bombers and airliners landing without crews; and of stranded flying machines saved by wandering strangers emerging from windstorms.

A few famous authors have hinted of similar stories. Richard Bach wrote about an inexplicable takeoff from an impossibly short field in an Aeronca Champ that defied all laws of physics. The great Ernest K Gann penned tales of Douglas DC-3s with apparent supernatural powers, steered by fate. The gifted writer, Antoine De Saint-Eupéry told of monstrous turbulence in the Andes and of being flung through violent mountain storms without control or consequence. And there was the factual story of Flight 401, an Eastern Airlines L-1011 that crashed in the Florida Everglades, killing 96 passengers and its cockpit crew. Ghosts of its pilot and first officer were seen by passengers and crew on other flights dozens of times, and once by a captain who was so shaken, he canceled an entire flight. The airline quietly removed equipment that had been salvaged from the crash and placed into other Eastern airplanes, and the apparitions were never seen again. It remains a great aviation mystery.

Supernatural events were common in the early days of aviation. In 1935 an otherwise ordinary pilot named Robert Victor Goddard was sent to inspect an unused airfield near Edinburgh, Scotland at a place called Drem. Goddard flew over in his biplane and reported that the base appeared dilapidated and unused, with cattle grazing on its cracked runways. Heading home, Goddard flew into a severe rainstorm that appeared without warning. He turned his biplane back toward Drem to land and wait the storm out. As he approached, the downpour turned to bright sunlight, and he again saw the base below. Only this time it was alive with mechanics and airplanes and pilots. But the aircraft he reported had not yet existed in 1935, nor had the uniforms he saw on the crews there. They were from World War II- an event that would not happen for another five years. He didn't land, unable to explain what he was looking at. Newspapers of the time reported the fantastic event. Goddard concluded he had been given a brief glimpse into the future.

The source of these experiences appears to be an odd corner of existence that we aviators are given access to maybe once in a lifetime. It's a privilege (or curse) we share with nobody else, except maybe the sailors of old who plied the seas in tall, wooden ships. They also told stories of ghost captains, mysterious winds, and disappearing islands, not all of which could be attributed to fever or too much rum.

It might have to do with our love affair with the flying machine itself. While the public sees our airplanes as inert machines made of wood and wire and metal, we aviators know they have a soul. We've often felt our machines communicating with us through their controls and their wings, sometimes responding to our mere thoughts. We can tell you if an airplane is a "he" or a "she," we know when our planes are ailing, and we sense their reluctance when we ask too much of them. We care for our airplanes with deep passion, polishing, repairing, and adjusting to the point of obsession. We speak to our aircraft, give them names, and spend untold hours with them and in them.

Sometimes we ask our flying machines to do the impossible, or to protect our precious cargo of family and loved ones. When they do just that, we respond with a pat on the airplane's spinner or a "thank you" mouthed in silence. We can feel the love from certain machines, and defiant stubbornness from others. Still, we feel something from all of them.

Pilots learn much about themselves in the cockpits of these airplanes. It has been said that an individual's purest personality is distilled within the confines of an airplane cockpit-especially in times of trouble. That is where many of us feel our greatest sense of accomplishment, joy, and sometimes, fear. The transformation pilots undergo as they become creatures of the sky is almost mystical.

I considered that this exceptional bond between man and machine—and the apparent alchemy it invokes— may unlock a portal that creates a kind of bridge between this life and the next. That portal is ephemeral, and none of us knows when or even *if* it will open. That veil between our world and the other is sometimes thin. Maybe it exists only in certain places, like the Bermuda Triangle, or a little corner of Fort Stockton, Texas. It's possible that it wanders in time and space, stopping here and there. Whatever the mechanism, a benevolent old mechanic had crossed over it to help us that day. Don and I knew we hadn't imagined our encounter- the new mechanical parts in our very real engine were proof of that. Our experience might have been one of those "things" that Shakespeare's Hamlet was referring to when he said, "There are more things in heaven and earth, Horatio, than are dreamt of in your philosophy."

My phone didn't ring again that night, and nothing more was ever discovered about the chief. I never found any more information about that wayward stranger who emerged from a windstorm to save two pilots and their little blue bird from certain disaster. Scouring my memories for any tidbit I might have missed about who this man was, I remembered the last thing he had said before he drove off into the night in his pickup truck: "I'll be here," he had smiled. "I'm always here."

The little Grumman at Fort Stockton.

Fairchild PT-19s on the Gibbs Field (Fort Stockton) flightline in January 1943.

(Historical photos courtesy of U.S. Army Air Force- public domain)

Gibbs Field terminal in 1943 and in 2021, with the "loaner" Ford Explorer parked out front. This grand old building has since been demolished.

Marc C. Lee is a lifelong pilot and writer. After earning his pilot certificate at seventeen, Marc worked for famed movie pilot Frank Tallman at his "Movieland of the Air" museum in California. Marc's aviation career included running his own flight school, flying as a commercial pilot, and teaching aviation both in the cockpit and the classroom. As a writer, Marc spent eight years as a contributing editor for Plane & Pilot magazine, and published articles in various genres around the world. He is a thirty-year member of the American Society of Composers, Authors, and Publishers (ASCAP), where he has twice received writer awards. As a songwriter, his compositions have been featured on radio, television, and in film. Marc is currently a director and script writer for a leading aviation course publisher. A longtime vintage airplane owner, Marc lives with his family in Southern California.

From Out of the Wind

Made in United States
Orlando, FL
01 September 2022

21807245R00052